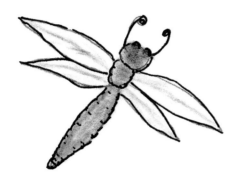

Emmojean's Tale

Written by Margaret Rose MacLellan

Illustrated by the Author & Jessica Schaaf

Jessica Schaaf

Margaret Rose MacLellan

4TH FLOOR PRESS

www.4thfloorpress.com

© 2018 Margaret Rose MacLellan

THIS BOOK IS A WORK OF FICTION AND IMAGINATION.

ISBN: 978-1-988993-04-1

Kindle (mobi): 978-1-988993-05-8

Kobo (epub): 978-1-988993-06-5

1st Printing 2018

Printed in Canada

Illustrations by the Author & Jessica Schaaf

forgetmenotexpressions@gmail.com

Dedication

My children, Heather, Jessica, and Angelina, my husband Doug,

and my parents, Walter and Irene,

I promised all of you that one day I would write a little tale,

... here it is with all my love.

An Introduction

Just Before the Story Begins –

Strolling down the garden path;

a place of puddles; the little birds' bath -

where vegetables and flowers grow in rows galore

among tiny rocks, little bugs, delightful smells, and more.

A special place, tucked away from the world of the large.

A peaceful place, where no bullies or mean ones are in charge.

And, so it was, within her grandma's garden, so beautiful, so sweet,

that a young girl's life changed one summer, by one she happened to meet.

For it was deep within her grandma's garden where,

one fateful summer's day, a young girl happened upon a faerie-tale creature, extraordinaire!

He was the most amazing being she had ever seen,

and when it happened … she had to pinch herself to make sure it was not a dream.

But, it was no dream that she was in,

it was a tale for the telling about to begin!

And, it all began one early summer's day, just before noon,

down at the pond, nestled in her grandma's garden, under all of them -

the sun, the stars, and the moon!

Chapter One

How It All Started – A Parting and A Meeting

Please forgive me for the gloomy start, but I have to tell it the way it really did happen …

It actually began sadly, as she watched, waving, as her parents drove away,

it was at her grandma's for the summer, once again she was to stay.

Through misty eyes, she thought about another summer away from them,

thinking, she bit her trembling lip and grabbed at her skirt hem.

It was down the garden path she broken-heartedly began to race,

her destination, the centre of her grandma's garden, where a pond filled the space.

She ran as fast as her legs would go,

what this summer would bring … at the moment, she didn't want to know.

Her tear-stained face felt the mid-morning's breeze;

when she reached the pond, she dropped, devastated, down to her knees.

She loved her grandma so very much,

but inside she ached, and at her heart she did clutch.

Filled with despair, her sadness moved her to weep,

it seemed the tears on the inside were the tears she would keep.

She thought to herself, "*Why must I be away from the ones I need most?*

To my parents, it seems to me, I am no more than a ghost."

Then, she spoke out loud, "Why can't they see what this is doing to me?"

and she cast her gaze upward, pleading, "I need my family!"

She searched through her mind and her heart, desperately looking for a clue,

but the questions remained on the inside, locked away, in the place where they grew.

Then, while she was aching and crying and pondering why,

she caught sight of something out of the corner of her eye.

Instantly, she was overtaken by a tingling magical sort of feeling,

and what she saw next sent her whole body reeling.

She stared, dropped-jaw, in a straight ahead direction,

focused her eyes on the pond, and blinked at an incredible reflection.

Her eyes slowly rose to meet an amazing sight,

all the while a faerie-tale figure cautiously, slowly, crept into the light.

He had hair that stood at once north, south, east, and west,

unruly red hair; twisting and turning in all directions at best.

He had an imp-like face on a head quite round

where, upon blushing cheeks, many tiny freckles were found.

While he appeared elf-like upon the very first sight,

he was a little small for an elf and, perhaps, more of faerie birth, by right.

He sported wings that shimmered in the sun's warm glow,

that quickly folded in, so having them, no one would ever really know.

Taken aback by the sight, she did not know what to say,

and this odd little creature looked at her, in a strange and similar kind of way.

He darted to the side to get out of her view,

but it was directly into the pond that his tiny frame flew.

She jumped to her feet and it was straight into the pond that she ran,

to rescue the little creature was her immediate plan.

She moved through the water like moving through mud in a troubled dream.

To reach the spot where he tumbled in would take forever, it did seem.

She reached for his small body as it began to sink to the pond's bottom,

the only feeling she wanted to feel right then, was the relief she'd feel, once she got him.

He was gasping and gripping and he actually pulled her long hair –

this panic-stricken, elven-faerie type boy who was so clearly rare.

She lifted him up, freeing him from the pond water's hold,

she trembled when she realized his very small body was so wet and so cold.

But, he sat straight upright in her cupped hand and he said with a grin –

"Why, if I'd have been just a tiny bit bigger, I'd have pulled you right in!"

She immediately grimaced and then she started to speak,

but he held up his small hand – her attention he did seek.

"I'd like to introduce myself on this morning – um, hum, .. so wet, yet so clear,

I am the elven-faerie Tumble-Linus and who … are you … my dear?"

"Why," she answered quite softly, although she hadn't really planned it,

"My name is Emmojean … Emmojean Granbandit."

Now, he started to chuckle and she wasn't impressed,

she tried to hold back her shock and upset with her best.

"What do you find so amusing about my name?" she pointedly asked.

"Well," he snickered, "your last name – 'Grand Bandit' - why it brings to mind the vision of an outlaw that's masked!"

"I will have you know, boy faerie with the hair so red,

that my name is an honourable one and I can assure you I am very well bred!"

"Oh," Tumble-Linus retorted, "while I know others talk about it, I don't really understand much about good breeding.

It's just your name having the word 'bandit' in it, why it's unusual and I am thinking … for you, at times … perhaps … a little trouble leading?"

"You rascal of a faerie, you rude little lad,

where are your manners?" she asked. "And why are you so bad?"

"I'm not bad, Emmojean," he said. "No sirree!"

"It's simply that, while I don't look for trouble, trouble seems to find me!"

He giggled. "I'm usually not in cold water, but in hot water instead."

As he spoke, he shook the wetness from his tangled hair; so troublesome, so red.

He sighed, wiping his brow. "Such is the burden and the fate of faerie-elves.

Yes, magnets to adventure spelled 't-r-o-u-b-l-e' is where we often find ourselves!"

She stared at the small figure, holding him gently, yet tight;

And, while he was soaking wet and small, he was certainly full of fight.

She softened and spoke in a voice quite absent of fear,

as she was now aware of a growing connection to the drenched little dear.

"I think I know how you feel, Tumble-Linus-faerie-elf,"

she sighed. "I really can't seem to steer clear of trouble myself!

You are right. Both of my names cause some talk among my peers,

but the names were given to me, through fathers and mothers, grandparents and beyond, passed down through the years."

Then, she sighed again, but in a more awkward, uncomfortable kind of way,

as images of the past school year in her head began to play.

She hadn't had the best time again at school this past year,

many of the days were filled with troubles, worries, and sometimes, fear.

It seemed she always had struggles to find and to keep her school friends.

Alone and lonely, each school year closed, leaving her with many loose ends.

Emmojean suddenly felt Tumble-Linus staring a stare that passed her right through.

She felt him reading her thoughts … oh … the things he could know … if he knew!

Emmojean started, "How about we get out of this pond as we are so very wet.

Let's move into the sun to warm and dry or it's colds we'll both get."

It was at that precise moment, on that fateful summer's day, very late in the morn,

that a very special friendship between human and elven-faerie was about to be born.

Chapter Two

The Muddle - Where the Troubling Trouble Comes to Light

They set themselves down in a nice sun-warmed spot

to dry off the pond's water that left them quite opposite of hot.

Emmojean was very curious about this wee, small lad

whom only moments earlier she was ready to declare completely and utterly 'bad.'

She looked at him, she squinted, but she looked at him merely.

He squinted right back, mimicking her, copying her clearly.

She bit her bottom lip in a pondering kind of way,

he winked, bit his bottom lip too—this little elven-faerie sure liked to play!

Emmojean started, "Do you always make fun? Do you always make jokes?"

He answered lightheartedly, "Only with long-haired human girl-type folks!"

There was a twinkle in his mystical, dancing green eyes,

eyes so stunning and sincere, they couldn't possibly tell lies.

They just stared at each other, holding fast, for a brief intermission,

then Tumble-Linus darted, turning around, changing his position.

He then shot up the nearest branch of the closest tree,

and said, "I need a better look at you, Emmojean, I really need to see!"

He balanced, lying on his stomach, on a branch, over Emmojean's head,

and he smiled and shook his mane of untamed hair still so wet and so red.

It was there in the tree where he decided to clear his voice to speak.

His was a voice of elven-faerie size; small, but certainly not weak.

"Emmojean, my dear, soaked, sad, newfound friend,

what is making you so unhappy, looking so like the world is nearing its end?"

Emmojean began to fill with all kinds of opposites in her feeling,

she felt she was being drawn toward a moment most revealing.

Tumble-Linus started to ask what seemed like question after question

and Emmojean tried to answer, but was overcome with confused answer congestion.

She sputtered as her words fumbled and began spilling forward from her mouth,

she was so embarrassed by this, that she cast her eyes south.

In her mind, she really did not know how or where to begin.

Tumble-Linus waited; lying on his stomach, his head resting on hands that supported his chin.

Emmojean shook her head, trying to clear it and make sure all of this was real.

His look was so honest, so encouraging, that her confusion slowly began to peel.

Emmojean began to let her story flow out and, as she let it unravel,

Tumble-Linus listened quietly, not stopping her, like an angry judge with a gavel.

She told him about how some of the kids at her school

taunted and tormented her because she just wasn't 'cool.'

She talked about how she was teased about her name being so 'weird' and her first name so 'out of date,'

and how she was harassed on her way to school many a time, causing her to be late.

She told him how some cajoled and kidded her about the way that she dressed,

and some of her peers made it public knowledge, that it was at 'nothing' she was the best.

She was always last to be picked on any of the school or class teams.

To be accepted by others was but a thin hope confined to her dreams.

Emmojean told Tumble-Linus that because she had no real friends,

that when each school year finished she was left at odds with the ends.

While the teachers seemed to like her, she still struggled to fit.

But, when she was feeling the most defeated, a voice inside her always screamed 'NEVER QUIT!'

Emmojean loved to dance and to draw, to paint and to write,

and she loved all these things completely; she loved them with all her might.

Inside, she knew that she could never give way, she could never give in

to do that would mean she would lose and her tormentors would win.

It wasn't that simple and she would never easily surrender;

as she was purpose-driven to peacefully overcome the offender.

It was when Emmojean moved on to talk about her parents that she cried,

she told Tumble-Linus about the love from her parents that she truly felt denied.

It was at this exact point that Tumble-Linus sat bolt upright with his green eyes nearly popping

straight out of his head,

"Are you kidding me, Emmojean, did I really hear what you just said?

Why I can tell you honestly and I can tell you truly,

your parents love you immeasurably and they care for you duly."

"Why then do they leave me?" Emmojean asked him quite squarely.

"Why is it that my summers are spent with them rarely?"

"Why Emmojean my dear, you poor, poor, darling child

to be left so long without an answer has caused your world to turn wild!

Maybe I can offer you something; a little insight into knowing?

Your parents leave you here because it's safe and healthy for your growing.

If you could see how sad your parents are as they turn away to leave,

you would know for certain that not having you with them causes them to grieve.

Now, let me go a little further in regard to your prior report

about the peers at your school, that to bullying they resort.

I, too, have been troubled by my own kind in a similar sort of way

as my peers have often made fun of who I am, what I do, and even what I say.

They tease me about my origin and my birthright as my size is really quite rare.

They say I am too big for a faerie, too small for an elf, but I refuse to get caught up in their nasty

snare.

For, I am who I am, and this troubles me not

for I believe every creature on thc planet has a right to a spot.

It is of no consequence what they say or what they think,

for while I may be unusual, each of us is different -- that's what makes us distinct.

So faerie or elf or somewhere in-between,

bothers me not, as all my life it is this way I have been!

No longer do the jokes, pokes, odd nods or prods of others making fun cause me any strife.

I was put here for a purpose—and that purpose is why I was given life.

My peers continue to tease me, especially about the most peculiar of my ... let's say ... talents

that is—when it comes to the simple matter of walking, well ... I become somewhat off-kilter,

and very off balance."

He lowered his voice to a whisper to say, "Let me show you as I tell you, and this I tell you very sincerely,

that whenever I start out to walk, why, my body goes into a rollicking tumble quite severely."

With this admission, he began to laugh and then he began to giggle

and, as he did this, his little elven-faerie tummy began to gently jiggle.

Then, all of a sudden, he jumped down from the tree with but one goal in mind,

to reveal to Emmojean the very thing about him, which his peers chose to be most unkind.

Emmojean waited in anticipation for the demonstration to get started.

When it did, what she saw made her laugh so hard she thought she'd be joining the dearly

departed.

Tumble-Linus stopped, stood, brushed himself off, and began to explain

that it was this very characteristic that inspired his nickname.

"However," he said, "I sincerely don't consider the naming a minus,

even though my peers have referred to it as 'The Major Flaw of Linus.'

Personally, I consider it an endowment, certainly a plus. Yes, indeed.

Did you know that such tumbling along could give one such remarkable speed!?

Why I can out-race animal, elf and faerie alike with this gift.

My peers are mistaken if they think this will be cause for a rift.

For me, it is an honour to have been given another name

as I stand out in a crowd of elves and faeries who may otherwise be content to be quite the same.

I do not want to be like every other faerie or elf.

I want to be 'Tumble-Linus.' Yes! I want to be myself!

I do not necessarily like hanging around with others who believe that to be included means a

test,

as some of these like to get involved in activities where outcomes aren't always the best.

Believe me, I can get into enough trouble all by myself.

I don't need an invitation to what's already great temptation for a faerie-elf.

So, instead, I come to this beautiful garden, this place of absolute delight

and I spend my time playing, resting, and pondering about how to make many things right.

I'd like to share something with you, Emmojean, and this I tell you very truly

I have some ideas that may help you with the school bullying unruly.

Often, to deal with these types, who won't let you rest,

you quite simply have to start by trying always to do and to be your best.

Your best is really quite easy, yes, quite easy, for you to be.

Let me offer you some pointers, that you, yourself, can try then see."

Emmojean's interest was now sharper than the needles on the surrounding needle trees,

so she settled in to listen, leaning forward, resting her elbows gently upon her knees.

Chapter Three

Mending and Fixing - The Magic of Believing

Tumble-Linus stood, stretching as much height as he could muster from his small size,

as he tried to smooth out the unruly red hair that refused to stay out of his eyes.

Then, with one hand behind his back and the other placed importantly across his chest,

he inhaled deeply, lifted his head proudly, and then, like a statesman, he professed:

"I have some words of wisdom that I have worked on through the years

that may make your life more comfortable and help to ease your fears.

These words I have carefully prepared for you, as not one point do I want to miss.

Dear Emmojean, my message for you is most sincere and it lovingly goes like this:"

As Tumble-Linus spoke, he made gestures with his hand in the air

and faerie dust glittered into the shape of the letters that he deposited there.

Listen to the voice inside; that is your inner guide telling you to stop and think before you do.

Offer your help to others; helping always makes at least two people happy – them and you.

Value your feelings as well as those of others; talk about them; never push or hide them away.

Empathize by showing you understand the feelings of others; show this in what you do and what you say.

You should be your own best friend; learn to accept, appreciate, and unconditionally love that friend.

Overlook the 'little things' as it is the bigger picture that is the most important in the end.

Unique describes everyone; understand that being unique often requires great courage to display.

Respect should be expected; you should expect to give it and to receive it every day.

Share your talents with others; you may very well inspire another to share their talents in return.

Encourage others wholeheartedly; this fuels success and leads others to achieve what they yearn.

Learn how others see things so you can appreciate the world through other peoples' eyes.

Find some good in each and every person, because in each and every one of us some good resides."

Then, with all the love in the world now filling Tumble-Linus' caring heart,

he uttered one last statement (which was his point right from the start).

"These words are not meant to be empty shells of hope just springing from my head.

I believe that love and happiness can grow from and be spread by these things just said.

LOVE YOURSELF

However, it is imperative, that first, and above all else,

before you can learn to love others, you must

first learn to accept and to love yourself."

Tumble-Linus then bowed his head and stepped carefully to the side,

Emmojean stared, open mouthed, for her amazement, she could not hide.

It was several moments before she was able to break the silence and to speak,

as she thought about this elven-faerie lad; how wise he was; how far he was from meek.

The faerie dust held the message only momentarily suspended in the air.

and the words "L O V E   Y O U R S E L F" sparkled and then, in a breath, disappeared to everywhere.

Emmojean, now feeling a comforting inner warmth, smiled to herself

as the message lingered inside her head she stared in awe at the faerie-elf.

 "Please tell me, Tumble-Linus, in order to help make things more clear for me to see,

and please don't think it rude me asking," she hesitated, "but how long have you known of me?"

"Well," he said, "I have lived far longer than you could ever really conceive,

but then, this is knowledge that isn't for just anyone to receive ..."

"Tell me," Emmojean interrupted, watching his eyes, which were now breathtakingly glowing,

"How is it that you come to my grandma's garden without me ever really knowing?"

Tumble-Linus thought to himself—he had come to know her because he had seen her in the past and he had seen her often.

He looked at her ready to speak and then his voice began to soften.

"I come here when I am needed most, but I am only seen by those,

who are truly ready to know me. Why, yes! That's it! Yes, that's it … I suppose.

You see, I've come here in summers past and, Emmojean, it is you I've been coming to know,

but until YOU really needed me and believed my existence possible; why, myself, I could never

ever show."

"Tumble-Linus, I must ask you," Emmojean said as she began to gather all the courage she could

muster,

"Were you sent to find me now to help sort out my life's current bluster?"

Tumble-Linus looked at Emmojean with a look that could melt the hardest heart.

"Emmojean, my dear, it is up to you to determine if I am to play a part."

Emmojean was surprised by
this incredibly sincere and frank
admission,
and in her heart she knew
she'd already made that very
important decision.

Then, suddenly, it dawned on her that this little fellow was very surely sent,

to help her sort out some bothersome things; to help her figure out what they all meant.

Now, Emmojean's sadness began to melt away and her gloominess turned to glee;

her world was turning brighter now, because she was clearly beginning to see.

This was going to be the most wonderful summer she could ever hope to spend

as she now realized she had found in Tumble-Linus, a new and true dear friend.

Chapter Four

Sorting Things Out - A Commitment and A Request

The summer winds blew through the hottest of

days,

then the rain pelted down on the thirsty garden,

offering some grace.

For nearly sixty days and sixty nights,

Emmojean stayed at her grandma's to her

grandma's absolute delight.

While she wanted so desperately and so dearly to

say

that she had found a magical friend in the garden

on that very first teary day;

and, while she wanted to blurt out that all the

wonders at the pond that summer season

had been made even more wondrous and exciting

for one special reason,

she had made herself a promise to be silent about her newfound friend,

a promise that she'd promised and one that she'd keep until the end.

Her grandma never really asked her what she did or where she spent each day.

She just smiled, hugged and kissed Emmojean in her all-knowing, grandmotherly kind of way.

As the days passed by and summer drew closer to an end,

Emmojean had to leave her grandma's and her newfound elven-faerie friend.

She had to return home and to the school where only months earlier she had felt so all alone.

Some of those thoughts, once recalled, caused her to shiver straight to the bone.

But, when her parents came to get her, Emmojean spoke to them about all the feelings she felt inside.

She put a value on her feelings; she pushed nothing to the side.

She told her parents that she felt rejected when they left her at her grandma's on her own;

how leaving her each summer made her think their hearts were made of stone.

She found out that her parents had no idea that their leaving her caused her to feel this way—

they comforted her and assured her that they loved her more and more with each precious passing day.

And Emmojean came to realize that to her parents she really wasn't 'just a ghost,'

Tumble-Linus was right—it was at her grandma's they left her because they knew she'd receive love and care the most.

Emmojean had decided that she would follow all that Tumble-Linus had suggested,

that she would be her best, do her best, and learn to love herself (as he had so eloquently requested).

Emmojean was returning home with an even more resolute and decided attitude.

She would show kindness and understanding to all, especially to those who had been so rude.

Before she left for home, Tumble-Linus told Emmojean he had 'something special' he wanted to give her

and he asked her to return in the late fall so that 'something special' he could deliver.

Emmojean promised to return when summer had folded into the deep coolness of late fall

to honour the wishes of Tumble-Linus—her newest and truest friend of all!

Chapter Five

A Gift and A Reminder

The time was all too soon upon them; the weather turned colder and with it, the pond's water

cooled to ice.

The leaves had changed from green to gold and fallen to the ground, making warm cozy beds for

the sleepy little mice.

The flowers had long since bloomed their last bloom, withered and drifted into winter sleep;

leaving behind a promise to return in spring and bloom blossoms so beautiful, that admiring

eyes would weep.

All the little bugs and insects, were now quietly nestled in,

hiding and sleeping; each little tiny face wearing a little tiny grin.

They left with the promise that they would be back again in the spring time, too,

to busy themselves doing the things that little bugs and insects do.

Tumble-Linus appeared at the pond one last time before retiring until spring.

He was on a mission, as he had promised Emmojean that he'd deliver that special thing.

He picked up a sturdy stick and climbed onto a low lying branch in a nearby tree

where, on the newly frozen pond's surface, he began to etch some words for Emmojean to see.

What he wrote for her leapt straight from his elven-faerie heart

as the bond he now had with Emmojean could never, ever be broken apart.

He etched with the stick upon the ice just three simple words,

the witnesses to this act were the winter animals and the cold weather birds.

Tumble-Linus simply wrote "Love - Yours - Elf" in the ice upon the pond

and he enclosed those words within a hand-drawn heart (a shape with which he had recently

grown quite fond).

Then, he jumped down from the wintry tree, and from his pocket he withdrew

a little heart-shaped locket, though it was quite shiny, it really wasn't new.

He placed the locket within the heart that encircled his short note;

a gift for Emmojean, he thought to himself, as a memory of what he wrote.

He was looking at the pond, from his position near the tree

when his attention was diverted, catching sight of Emmojean—nearing very quickly.

As Emmojean had not yet seen him, he drew out his wings and swiftly flew out of her sight.

Tumble-Linus wanted so desperately to be going; he wanted to take flight.

He really didn't want to see her because he really didn't want to cry.

But, as he watched her drawing nearer, he felt the tears moving straight from the heart to the

eye.

Now an elven-faerie has the special magic to quickly disappear completely out of view,

especially when he's an elven-faerie who's been around a year or two!

Tumble-Linus made himself vanish from Emmojean's line of sight,

while inside his heart was heavy, as he held back an ocean of tears with all his might.

Emmojean began to run towards the pond, looking for a sign from her newest, dearest friend

and, when she reached the pond she knew at once, he had been true to her to the end.

There she saw the message written in the ice so cool and clear

and she leaned over closer to read the message left by the little dear.

"Oh my," Emmojean whispered as she knelt down and picked up the heart-shaped locket,

at once, the real message he had left for her met her with the impact of a rocket.

She clasped the locket to her chest and raised her face toward to the skies,

she stretched both of her arms upward as the tears streamed downward from her eyes.

"Tumble-Linus," she said, "my dearest, best and truest friend,

your message holds the key to the magic that has now gone beyond this summer's end.

What you mean for me to know right now comes from the very heart of a faerie-elf,

your meaning becomes so clear, Tumble-Linus—it is simply—"**Love Yourself**."

She desperately looked all around her in hopes that she would find him near.

She wanted to share the positive experiences that she was having at school so far this year.

Emmojean wanted to tell him that she was practicing all he had said

and that things were working out much better and she was feeling far less dread.

She was committed to making peace by approaching her school challenges with love and an open heart.

She showed her courage and resolve by confiding in her teacher, who offered help right from the telling moment's start.

She really wanted to share her new school experiences with Tumble-Linus right then and there and, while she could not see him, she felt in her heart that he was already quite aware.

Tumble-Linus did know these things and as he watched her from his position quite invisible and secure,

he sadly wondered if she would see him again--about this, he was selfishly hopeful, but really not quite sure.

But, in his heart, there was one thing about which he was truly unmistaken—

Emmojean was so full of goodness, that her stalwart spirit could not be shaken.

He watched her turn her back to him and, as she made her way to leave,

she tried to wipe away her sadness, mopping up bittersweet tears with the corner of her sleeve.

Chapter Six

Wrapping It All Up – Coming Full Circle

Emmojean returned to her grandma's house and put her coat upon the shelf.

Then, she delicately placed around her neck, the treasure from the faerie-elf.

As her grandma came to greet her, she stopped and stood rigid in her place,

a look of utter surprise and amazement came swiftly across her face.

She looked at the locket closely and touched it with her finger,

thoughts swarmed within her head and there they began to linger.

She admired the lovely locket with its timeworn and faded shine,

"Wherever did you come across this treasure?" she asked. "This locket, oh, so fine?"

"Why, I found it down at the pond," Emmojean answered, "it was just moments ago that I

happened upon it."

"I really can't believe my eyes," her grandma said, withdrawing a tissue from her apron pocket.

She began to speak, smiling warmly, as she started recalling from the past

a memory among stored memories, which was necessarily meant to last.

She began, "One summer many years ago, when I was just a child,

there was a period in my life when things around me were a little unsettled, just a little bit wild.

I used to find refuge in a very special place, a place that I was to become quite fond.

That world was where I lost a locket. It was a place down by the pond."

"Yes," she remembered, "that summer was surely the most amazing one for me

because it was that particular summer I learned how to set some troubling troubles free.

It was that summer," she reminisced, "that I learned something so important to the self.

It was the summer I learned a very important life lesson, how before you can truly love others,

you must learn to accept and to love yourself."

Emmojean's grandma looked so incredibly radiant; her face now beautifully aglow,

Emmojean was quite beside herself -- was it really possible for her dear grandma to also know?

"Why grandma, please tell me," Emmojean encouraged. "Please, tell me do,

what happiness bringing thing that summer was introduced to you?"

"Well," her grandma began again, "I learned that when things are troubling you and troubling

you truly,

that sometimes wonderful things can come along to guide and help you cope with those things

unruly."

Her grandma began to recite the words and phrases that Emmojean had so recently heard.

Emmojean closed her eyes remembering; remembering the sight, remembering every word.

Listen Offer Value Empathize,

You Overlook Unique Respect Share Encourage Learn Find

It was at that moment that Emmojean and her grandma came to an unspoken bond of knowing;

each hugged the other; a symbol; sealing their shared understanding and a love ever-growing.

And, all the while, just outside the window overlooking grandma's garden in a newly snow-covered needle tree,

sat a heart-warmed Tumble-Linus looking on with a smile of reverie!

He snuggled himself and he huggled himself and then he resolutely did say,

"This could not have ended in a better, more wonderfully, wonderful kind of way!"

And, with those words he smiled, and through the snow he began to walk then he tumbled along in turn,

as his thoughts moved toward the coming spring, when to grandma's garden he would return!

♥♥   The End   ♥♥

About the Author

Margaret Rose MacLellan

Margaret Rose MacLellan is a Canadian writer, and this is her first published piece. This tale has been a long time in the making and a true labour of love which she is now delighted to share with you. Margaret is a mother of three grown children and currently resides in Calgary, Alberta, with her husband Doug, a cat named Azizzi and a bird named Mia.

forgetmenotexpressions@gmail.com